D1129552

LITTLE RED

LITTLE RED

PEARL S. BUCK

Illustrated by

DUANE KRYCH

CREATIVE EDUCATION, INC MANKATO, MINN

Published by Creative Education, Inc. 123 South Broad Street,
Mankato, Minnesota 56001

Printed in the United States of America.

Library of Congress Cataloging-in-Publication Data

Buck, Pearl S. (Pearl Syndenstricker), 1892-1973.
Little Red.

(Creative's classic short stories)

SUMMARY: In China during World War II, a young boy makes a daring rescue attempt to free his father, a captured prisoner of the Japanese army.

1. China — History — 1937-1945 — Juvenile fiction.
[1. China — History — 1937-1945 — Fiction.
2. Courage — Fiction. 3. Fathers and sons — Fiction]
I. Krych, Duane, ill. II. Title. III. Series.
PZ7.B879Lj 1987 [Fic] 87-8962
ISBN 0-88682-124-X
Mankato, MN: Creative Education: 32 p.

To the continuation and preservation
of short stories for readers
of all ages

Little Red was called Little, because his father was Big Red, and he was called Red because, like his father, he always wore something red. Big Red and Little Red, father and son, had always lived, since they were born, in a village on the edge of a small lake in the mountainous country of Lu, in the province of Kiangsi, in China.

The reason the two, father and son, so loved the color red was a simple one. Big Red had been the only son of his mother, and for that reason she kept him dressed in red until he was too big, and then she gave him a red kerchief to wear around his neck.

"I can see you a long way off," she always said,

"because of the red kerchief."

So Big Red grew up wearing the red kerchief.

When Little Red was born, he looked exactly like his father, and his mother, who was a sweet and gentle woman, was the first to see this. She loved Big Red, and as a sign of her joy in the little son, she kept him dressed in red until he was too big, and then she gave him a red kerchief, but a little one.

"I can always see where you both are, father and son, Big and Little, with your red kerchiefs," she said.

It was true that when the farmers were working in their fields she could see her two, and when they went to town she could see them coming home, for when she looked out of the door there were the two spots of red, which were their kerchiefs.

They lived happily in the village until the Japanese came, and they never even imagined that someday an enemy would come and take their beautiful country. Some people might have called them poor, for no one in the village had ever seen an automobile, much less owned one, and the houses were small; and none of the fathers ever had much money in his pockets. On the other hand, some people would have called them rich, for they had good food to eat, rice and vegetables, and very fine fish, and chickens and pork, and certainly the best

eggs. And they had clothes enough to keep them warm in winter, and in summer Little Red and his playmates went swimming in the ponds, or they climbed the mountains behind the village and spent the day exploring. In autumn they gathered chestnuts from the trees on the mountains and roasted them over charcoal. Altogether it was a good life.

When the Japanese came it changed so quickly that it was hard to believe that it was the same place. The village had been such a safe and pleasant one, where babies played in the street, and where mothers sat in the doorways sewing and watching and talking to one another and laughing at what their children did. As soon as school was over, the school children played in the street, too, and Little Red was always one of them. They played hopscotch and shuttlecock and toss-pennies, and then skipped home to early suppers, and if there were actors in town visiting, they might go to a play in the temple court afterward.

It was as pleasant as that one day, and the next day all was changed. The villagers had heard something about the war, of course. People in the village did not read newspapers, but they listened to other people traveling by, and they heard about the Japanese and they wanted to take the whole of

China. But almost as soon as they heard it, it really happened. For the next day the whole village was in confusion. An army of men came tramping through. Some of the men were on foot, but some rode in the cars which the village had never seen. Little Red happened to be home from school for lunch, and he had taken his bowl to the door and stood eating as fast as he could because he wanted to get back to school in time to play before afternoon work began. He was pushing rice and cabbage into his mouth with his chopsticks when suddenly he felt his father pull his shoulders, jerk him back, and slam the door shut and bar it.

Inside the house everything went wrong at once. His father dropped his bowl on the tile floor and broke it, his mother spilled the tea she was pouring, and the baby began to cry.

"The dwarfs are really here," Big Red gasped to Little Red's mother.

"You must run out of the back door up the mountain," she gasped back. "You should have gone yesterday with the other men, when we first heard the dwarfs were near."

"I did want to get the cabbage planted before I went away," he groaned, "so that if I didn't get back you would have something to eat with the rice."

Before anything could be done, there was a great

noise and clatter at the door.

"Shall I open the door, Father?" Little Red asked.

Before anyone could open the door it crashed in, and there stood the strange men who were Japanese. Big Red and Little Red and the mother and the baby could only stare at them. They were all terrified, and the baby was so frightened that he stopped crying, his mouth wide open.

"You," one of the men yelled at Big Red. He was an officer and he carried a sword as well as a pistol. "Come out here! We want able-bodied men to carry loads for us!"

The moment he spoke the soldiers behind him seized Big Red by the hands and legs and jerked him out in the street. There was already a long line of villagers tied together with ropes, and to this long line Little Red now saw his father tied too. He ran and clung to his father's waist, and his father bent and whispered in his ear, "Get back into the house, bar the door, and take care of your mother!"

He dared not disobey his father, and yet how could he bear to see him go? He obeyed and he disobeyed. He ran into the house, barred the door, and ran out the back door again. There from a distance he watched what happened to his father. The line of villagers was driven down the road like oxen, and the enemy soldiers whipped them if they

went too slowly and pricked them with their bayonets. At the head of the line Little Red saw his father march steadfastly away southward. Hiding himself in the bushes, he followed until he was sure of their road, and then he ran home to tell his mother.

You can imagine how his mother cried when she heard what had happened to Big Red. She put the baby in his crib and sat down on a bench in the kitchen and cried and cried, wiping her eyes on her blue cotton apron.

"We will never see him again," she sobbed. "He is such a big strong man, he is so good, he is such a fine worker, they will never let him go. And now he is a prisoner! Oh, if I had only made him go to the mountains yesterday."

"What is in the mountains, Mother?" Little Red asked.

Then his mother told him, "In the mountains there are men from many villages gathering together in an army to fight the enemy. They wanted your father to come yesterday and lead them, and he promised to go as soon as the enemy drew near. This morning, even, he might have gone and been safe if he had not stayed to plant those wretched cabbages. How can I eat them now? They would choke me, for it is because of them he is taken prisoner."

Little Red listened to all of this and said nothing.

He was at this time twelve years old and he knew that there are times when it is better for a boy to listen and say nothing, especially when he is planning something very big. He let his mother cry until she was tired, and he held the baby when that small one began to fret, and he burned the grass under the caldron in the stove when his mother stopped crying after a long time and sighed and said, "Well, I suppose we must eat, even if he is gone. But you eat—I can't eat a thing."

She was rather astonished when he ate an unusually big supper, and she was inclined to be a little cross with him for it. "I am glad you have a big appetite," she said, "but I am suprised, when you know how your poor father is suffering."

He still said nothing. He went to bed very early and so did she, and they had not opened the door since he barred it shut at noon. The mother had cried so much that she went to sleep, although she had not thought she could. But Little Red did not sleep. In his bed he had put a bit of broken brick, and he lay with it in the middle of his back. He lay a long time thus, purposely to keep awake, and when at last he began to hear his mother breathe as though she were sound asleep he rose and made ready to carry out his plan. In his belt he thrust the kitchen chopping knife. In his red kerchief he tied some bread, rolls, and salted cabbage, and two hard-boiled salted duck eggs, which his mother always kept on hand. Then he felt in the broken teapot and took out half of the family money which they kept there. It was never very much, but he thought half would be enough for him in case he did not get home for a long time.

He wished that he could tell his mother where he was going, but she could not read, and there was no use in writing her a note. So he had to go without a word.

He opened the back door and slipped through. The moon was bright and better than any lamp, but he walked softly just the same. He had a long way to go and he set out swiftly and steadily southward. He knew exactly what he was going to do. He was going to find out where his father was, and with the knife he would cut the ropes that bound him and help him to get away.

He thought exactly how it would go. They would have to stop for the night somewhere. Probably the prisoners would all be lying on the ground. Of course they would be guarded by the soldiers. But he would creep forward carefully, making use of every shadow. Perhaps there might be a shadow over the moon by then to help him. Often enough clouds came out of the mountains in the night and spread up over the sky. But the sky was clear now.

He had never been out in the night alone before and he did not like it very well. The frogs were croaking loudly in the ponds, and a bird wailed out of a bamboo grove. But he went on. Two hours passed and he came at last to a village, where he hoped to find his father. It was empty. On the silent street every door was barred. His dream of finding Big Red there was only a dream.

He was so tired that for a moment he was discouraged. Where now should he turn?

But if they were going south, his reason told him, they would still be going south.

He got down on his knees and looked at the road in the bright moonlight. Like all the roads of that province, it had a stone path down the middle, made of flat stones from the mountains and polished smooth by people's feet. If many people had walked down the road today the dust would be tramped away and it would be sign of which way his father had gone. Sure enough, the polished stone was smooth and clean of dust. He got up again and followed it. When the road forked he followed the one which was clean of dust upon its stone path. It led steadily south.

Now Little Red knew that if you keep going south far enough you reach the great river, and if the prisoners and his father reached the river they would be put on boats, and then there would be no way of following them, for the water could give him no hint and no clue. He began to run instead of walk, dogtrotting along on his tired feet.

I must take the nearest way to the river port! he thought.

He had been to the river port twice with his father, because that is where the fair is held every year, and he knew the way. But of course the gates of the city would be locked at such an hour, and a country boy with a red kerchief full of bread and cabbage and two duck eggs would certainly not be let in or even listened to if he knocked.

There's nothing to do but go around the city, Little Red now told himself.

So he went around the city to the river's edge and crawled along in the mud for a long way. The city came right down to the river, and he had to step into the water to get past, but he did that easily enough, and was indeed quite ready to swim if the water were deep. But at this season the river was low, and he was able to walk around the wall.

Now he knew that the boats were all tethered to iron rings fastened in the stones of the river wall on either side of steep stone steps that went to the river, and so to the steps he went. There was not a sign of anyone. The moonlight shone down on the wet steps, and the quiet boats bobbed up and down on the slight swell of the river, and the whole city slept.

He had a dreadful moment of dismay. Suppose they had not come here at all! Perhaps he had guessed entirely wrongly! Then he remembered that he had come around the city, and they perhaps would come another way. And he had come quickly, being alone, and they would come slowly. He sat down on a corner of the step and made himself very small, and waited. He was so hungry that although he tried not to, he felt compelled to eat a piece of the bread he had brought for his father, but he would not allow himself to eat one of the duck eggs.

Scarcely had he done this when he heard a loud noise in the city. Shots rang out in the night, men yelled and cursed, and he heard the heavy squeak of the city gates.

I am right, he thought wildly. I shall see my father! And he squeezed himself very small against the wet wall, into a shadow which the parapet just above his head cast down on the steps. The red kerchief of food he hid between his knees.

Sure enough, in a few minutes of heartbeats so loud that they sounded in his ears like drums, he saw the weary line of men drag themselves around the corner. His father was still at the head of them. He knew his father, for he held up his head, and besides there was the red kerchief about his neck, clearly to be seen in the white moonlight. It was all Little Red could do not to call out, not to press forward. But he knew this would never do. So he sat small and close in the shadow.

It was well he did, for now the soldiers rushed after the prisoners and herded them down the steps together, and Little Red lost sight of his father entirely. A soldier brushed past him as he hurried down to the boats, and for a moment he was terrified. The soldier looked down at him, saw him, and gave him a kick and then went on. Little Red sat motionless while the prisoners were pushed on the boats.

Now he was glad that his father was Big Red. For he watched the spot of red on the tall man who got into the boats with all the others. Then Little Red put down his kerchief but he kept the knife in his belt, and silently, as the boats left the shore, he crept down the steps. Into the water he went as cleanly and deeply as one of the river animals that live along the shores of rivers. He paddled softly after the boats

and after the big man who sat on the edge of one of them, his red kerchief fluttering in the night wind.

The boats were rowboats, sampans, and small cargo boats, and the men to whom they belonged rowed slowly and unwillingly, knowing that they would get no pay for what they did. It was not too hard for Little Red to paddle along like a small dog and reach the side of the boat where Big Red sat, his head in his hands, tied to the other prisoners by the rope around his waist. Little Red dared not call. He hung onto the boat by one hand and with the other he reached for the knife and slipped it to his father's foot. Then he pounded lightly on that foot.

Big Red looked down from under his hands. He saw a kitchen knife—nothing else. Then he saw something bob up out of the water, a dark, wet little face. He could not see who it was, and before he looked again the head was bobbing away toward the shore.

For Little Red had very sensibly reasoned that he would go back and wait on the steps so that his father would have only himself to save. Purposely he did not let his father see who he was.

If he knows it is I, he thought, he will stay to see that I am all right and then maybe we'll both be caught.

So he took care of himself and dragged himself

out of the river and sat on the steps, very wet and a little cold. The red kerchief was still there, to his joy, for he had been afraid a dog might find it. The food smelled delicious, and he had to be very stern with himself and not even open the kerchief lest he eat more of it. He simply sat and waited.

Big Red, when he saw the knife, could not imagine how it had got there. If he had believed in strange things as some people did, he would have said a river god had come to his help. He was so astonished that he was almost ready to believe it. But he knew that he must not waste time wondering. He took the knife, which was very sharp, and softly cut his ropes. Then quietly he laid it on the foot of the next man and slipped into the water without a ripple. It was easy enough, for the boat was so laden with prisoners that its side was almost level with the river. He sank under the water and began to swim, holding his breath as long as he could. And then one of those clouds came out of the moutains, as they so often did just before dawn, and covered the face of the setting moon. When he came up again he was quite safe. No one could have seen his dark head against the muddy water of the river.

Little Red sat in the darkness on the steps and shivered. Now he could not see his father and he must listen carefully. Yes, in a few moments he heard a man breathing heavily and trying not to breathe. He called out softly, "My father!"

There was no answer. The breathing stopped suddenly. His father was afraid. Little Red understood at once.

"Big Red!" he whispered loudly. "It is Little Red!"

"Little Red?" his father whispered. "Then where are you?"

Feeling for each other along the step, they found one another and each gave the other a big hug.

"Why, you Little Red," his father gasped in a whisper. "How did you come here?"

"I brought the kitchen knife," Little Red whispered back.

But Big Red did not stop while he listened. With the father's arm about his son's shoulder, they went around the city wall and struck over a narrow path to the hills. And all the time Little Red told his father exactly what had happened, and Big Red laughed and hugged Little Red and said over and over again, "You see why the enemy can never conquer our country—no country can be conquered whose boys are like you!"

When they had reached the mountains they went into a little cave and now they felt safe.

"Here is the food," Little Red said proudly. Then

he felt he must tell the worst. "I did eat one piece of bread because I was so hungry," he confessed, "but I would only allow myself to have a duck egg."

His father took the kerchief and opened it and divided the food exactly into half. "You are a brave man," he said, "and brave men must eat. Moreover, they must share equally all that they have."

So they ate, and Little Red ate the duck egg, and it tasted even better than he had imagined.

"Now," his father said when they had eaten. "I must go up higher into the mountains and stay there."

"Oh," cried Little Red. "Let me come with you, Father!"

At this Big Red looked grave. "Who will look after the family?" he asked.

It was now Little Red who looked grave. "I should so much like to live in the mountains," he begged, "with you, Father! Because the baby keeps me awake at night when he cries."

His father laughed and clapped him on the shoulder. "Now," he said, "here's a compromise. You shall be the messenger between home and mountains. One night at home, one night in the mountains—how is that? Messengers we must have."

And that is how Little Red became what he is today, a messenger between the men on the plains and the men in the mountains. He stops often to see how his mother and the baby are, but he never stays more than one night. But sometimes by coaxing his father he stays a couple of nights and more in the mountains in an old ruined temple, where the villagers have made a fort. From there they go down into the valley and fight the enemy, and, as often as he can, Little Red tells them where the enemy is. He is too young to enlist, but how can Big Red do without him?

Pearl S. Buck
1892-1973

Pearl Buck said that she was as much Chinese as she was American. Born in West Virginia, her missionary parents took her to China a few months later.

Pearl grew up living among the Chinese. Rather than live in a missionary compound, her parents chose to live among the native people, in a small city on the Yangtze River. Each day, Pearl's mother taught her English, and in the afternoons her Chinese tutor came. When she was eighteen, she went to the United States to attend Randolph-Macon Woman's College in Virginia.

After graduating from college, she returned to China. Three years later she married John Lossing Buck, an American agricultural specialist. For the next five years she and her husband lived in a farming village in northern China. Pearl grew to love and admire the Chinese peasants and wanted to write about them. But she didn't have enough confidence yet to do it.

Then Pearl and her husband moved to Nanking, where they both taught at the University. There was much unrest in China at that time. In 1927 revolutionary armies invaded Nanking, and Pearl and her family had to flee for their lives.

Pearl's personal life created problems for her also. It was difficult for her to raise her mentally retarded daughter while she was trying to launch a writing career. Pearl soon found a way, however, to borrow some money and send her daughter to a special school for two years. This gave Pearl time to write. In a short time, her novel *The Good Earth* was published, and it brought her the Pulitzer Prize in 1932.

In 1934 she returned to the United States to live. She continued to write a steady stream of fiction, and won the Nobel Prize for Literature in 1938. She founded the East and West Association for the purpose of increasing understanding among the peoples of the world. Pearl adopted nine children of different nationalities and founded two agencies for the aid and adoption of Asian-American children. Her concern was always for children, "not because of a maternal instinct," she said, "for you know I am not a very maternal woman, but because children are the future."

This book was designed by Bill Foster and typeset by House of Graphics, St. Paul, Minnesota.

It is typeset in CG Times.

The color separations were done by The John Roberts Printing Company, Minneapolis, Minnesota.

Worzalla Publishing Company, Stevens Point, Wisconsin did the printing and binding.